W9-AAJ-013

For Katy Gall – Queen of all Stockport – RC

First published in Great Britain by Bloomsbury Publishing Plc.

Printed in Mexico
First Edition
1 3 5 7 9 10 8 6 4 2
This book is set in 26-point Goudy Infant.
Thomas, Frances, 1943-
What If?/Frances Thomas and Ross Collins, [illustrator].-1st ed.
p. cm.
Summary: Mother Monster soothes Little Monster with a pleasant story when he imagines a scary day.
ISBN 0-7868-0482-3
[1. Monsters-Fiction. 2. Imagination-Fiction. 3. Mother and child-Fiction.] I. Collins, Ross, ill. II. Title.
PZ7.T36665Wh 1999
[E]-dc21 98-39976

What If?

Frances Thomas and Ross Collins

Hyperion Books for Children

"Mom,"
said Little Monster.

"What if when I
woke up tomorrow morning
... there was a
big . . . black . . .

in the middle of the floor.

And I didn't want to fall in, so I called you and you didn't answer.

And then what if the hole got bigger and bigger and it was all dark and smelly.

And then there was a big, big spider and it got closer and closer.

And then there wasn't a ceiling and the sky was all horrible and I fell down

and down

and down.

And what if you couldn't come and help me because you had gone away.

And then the house caught on FIRE!

And the fire was all around me when I was falling down the hole.

And the spider was falling, too

And I couldn't see the bottom of the hole

And I just went on falling
forever and ever and ever.

Mom, what if all that happened when I woke up tomorrow, what would it be like?"

"Mmm," said Mother Monster, "that would be very scary.

But then what if tomorrow when you woke up, you called me and I was making pancakes.

And what if you ate up all your pancakes,

And then we went for a walk.

And what if we walked and walked until we found a green hill.

And at the bottom of the hill was an old man with a long red scarf, selling balloons.

And what if I bought a red balloon like a red jewel,

And you bought a green balloon like the green sea,

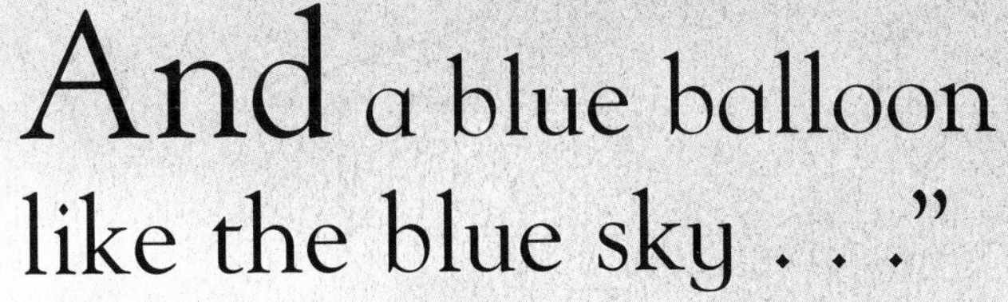

And a blue balloon
like the blue sky . . .”

“And a purple balloon,”
said Little Monster, “like . . .
like a lovely purple balloon.”

“Like a lovely purple balloon,”
said Mother.

"And then what if you and I climbed all the way to the top of the hill, and we stood there in the sun,

And then I let my red balloon float away and away into the sky. And then you let your blue balloon float away and away and your green balloon."

"Only not my purple balloon," said Little Monster. "I would take my purple balloon back home with me."

"Oh yes," said Mother Monster. "We'd take your purple balloon home.

But then on the way we'd meet an old man with a long yellow scarf, selling ice cream. And what if you had strawberry and I had chocolate . . ."

"Or the other way around?" said Little Monster.
"Or the other way around," said Mother Monster.

"And what if we walked home eating our ice cream and just as we'd finished, it was getting dark, but we got home,

And what if we went inside and made a fire and some toast . . ."

"And you'd tell me a story," said Little Monster.
"And I'd tell you a story. Would you like that?"
"Mmm," said Little Monster, "that would be very nice."

Then Little Monster said,
"What if I took my purple
balloon up to bed with me?
And it floated up to the ceiling
and stayed there ALL NIGHT
and didn't fall down?"

"Mmm," said Mother.
"That would be very, very nice."